15x2/15, J 5/14

Love, Lizzie

Letters to a Military Mom

Lisa Tucker McElroy

Illustrated by

Diane Paterson

Dear Mommy,
I miss you

Albert Whitman & Company
Morton Grove, IL

For Zoe and Abby, who hold the map to my heart.—L.T.M.

For my courageous daughters, Betsy and Jana.—D.P.

Acknowledgments: Many thanks go to Laaren Brown, for reading multiple versions of this manuscript; Selma Moss-Ward and the Thursday night Women's Writing Group, for listening to me brainstorm the concept; Abby Levine, a terrific and patient editor who was always ready to incorporate my ideas; Lt. Col. Jon Shelburne in the United States Marine Corps Reserve; Douglas Ide, Public Affairs Officer, U.S. Army Community and Family Support Center; Dr. Christina Bellanti, for helping me understand the issues families face when a parent is deployed; Scott Gerber in the Washington, D.C., office of Senator Dianne Feinstein, for his interest in this project and assistance with the foreword; and to Steve, Zoe, and Abby McElroy, for their love and support.

Library of Congress Cataloging-in-Publication Data

McElroy, Lisa Tucker.
Love, Lizzie : letters to a military mom / by Lisa Tucker McElroy ; illustrated by Diane Paterson.
p. cm.
Summary: Nine-year-old Lizzie writes to her mother, who is deployed overseas during wartime, and includes maps that show her mother what Lizzie has been thinking and doing. Includes nonfiction tips for helping children of military families.
ISBN 0-8075-4777-8 (hardcover)
[1. Military service, Voluntary—Fiction. 2. War—Fiction. 3. Mothers and daughters—Fiction. 4. Sex role—Fiction. 5. Women soldiers—Fiction. 6. Letters—Fiction.] I. Paterson, Diane, 1946- ill. II. Title.
PZ7.M478454234Lov 2005 [Fic]—dc22 2005003892

The design is by Carol Gildar.

For more information about Albert Whitman & Company, please visit our web site at
www.albertwhitman.com.

Today, and every day, there are many children in America like Lizzie, whose parents are posted overseas, making a personal sacrifice in leaving their children and families behind. In her letters to her mother, Lizzie speaks for all such children as she asks some important questions about war and patriotism: How long does defending freedom take? Why do you have to be away from me? Why can't you come home and be a part of birthdays, first days of school, and soccer championships? When will we be together again?

What do we want children like Lizzie to know? *Love, Lizzie* may ask difficult questions, but it communicates some important lessons as well: although our troops are overseas, they are always in our minds and hearts; we believe in and support the people fighting this war; and although parents are serving overseas, they are always remembering and loving their children and families. Parents in the military may temporarily look different—they wear helmets and boots, not sneakers and baseball caps; they may not be able to give hugs, but they can send wishes through the stars; they may be far away, but they always hold the maps to their children's hearts.

Love, Lizzie fills a need for all American children in this time when the world can sometimes feel full of terror and insecurity, war and uncertainty. In *Love, Lizzie*, children find hope and connection, patriotism and love. Lizzie's relationship with her mother—and her mother's service to America—are an inspiration to us all.

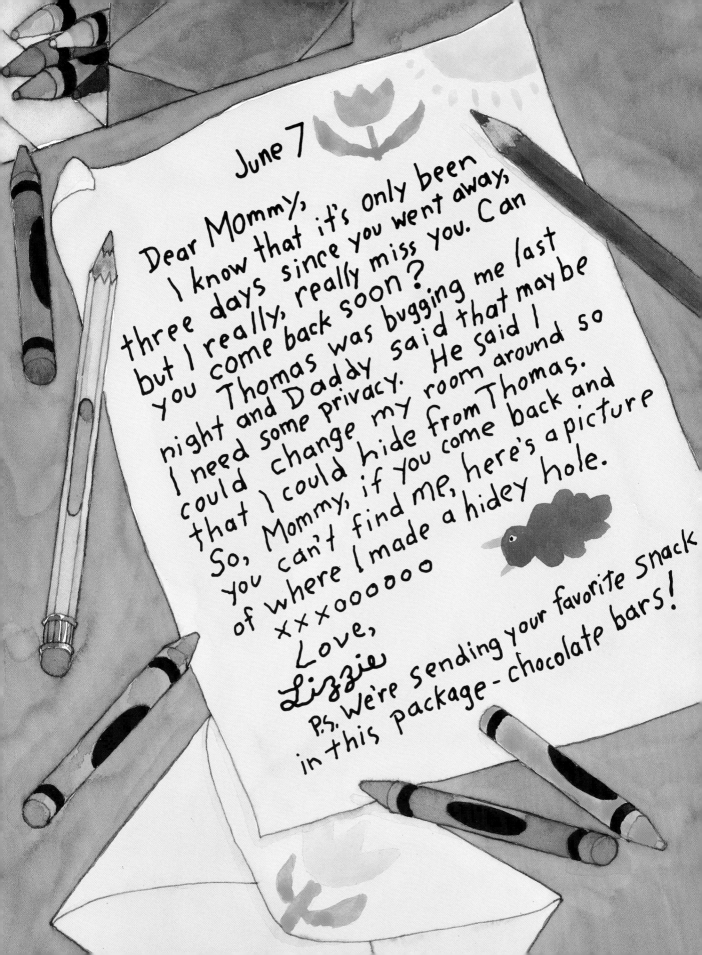

June 7

Dear Mommy,
I know that it's only been three days since you went away, but I really, really miss you. Can you come back soon?
Thomas was bugging me last night and Daddy said that maybe I need some privacy. He said I could change my room around so that I could hide from Thomas. So, Mommy, if you come back and you can't find me, here's a picture of where I made a hidey hole.
xxxoooooo
Love,
Lizzie

P.S. We're sending your favorite snack in this package—chocolate bars!

August 4

Dear Mommy,

It feels like you've been gone a really long time. How long does defending freedom take?

Thomas grew again and we had to get him some new pants. I'm going to grow my bangs out until you're here to trim them again.

Mrs. Cooperman next door sits for us after day camp till Daddy comes home. I wish she'd let us climb trees, but she says it's not safe. It's not fair, Mommy! You always let me climb trees!

Oh, but you know something so cool? There's a new ice cream store down the street! When you get home you'll know which one it is because it has a sign that says "Support Our Troops." Here's a map of where everything is — ice cream, my new friend Sarah's house, the pool — pretty much our whole neighborhood!

I love you, Mommy. I ate some Star-Spangled Strawberry for you. See you soon (I hope!!!!!!).

Covered in ice cream,

Lizzie

October 12

Dear Mommy,
I liked the email and the photo you sent yesterday— it's weird to think of you wearing a helmet and boots every day!
Mommy, our soccer team won the regionals! I got three goals in the semi-finals, and the team put me up on their shoulders! I'm sending the photo Daddy took of Sarah and me in our uniforms.
At the end of the month, we're going to the state finals on a school bus together- parents and everything. I really want you to go, too, Mommy. Can you ask if you can come home just for the game? If you don't get home in time, meet us there, OK?
I wish you could have seen me get the goals. It wasn't as much fun without you there.
Your superstar daughter,
Lizzie

November 24

Dear Mommy,
   Happy Turkey Day from Grandma and Grandpa's in Florida! I love the beach! Thomas and I buried Daddy in the warm sand yesterday, all the way up to his neck.
   It was a looooong trip to get here, Mommy. We had to take two planes! Daddy told me to look out the window when the pilot announced what we were flying over. Here's a map I drew. I could really see things like a bird does!
   Is there warm sand where you are, Mommy? I'm putting a little in this letter just in case.
   Fly home soon, Mommy,

Lizzie
   P.S. Are you staying safe, Mommy? Please don't forget to wear your helmet. I promise I'll wear my bike helmet EVERY TIME if you wear your helmet, too- Ok?

December 10

Dear Lizzie,
   It was so great to hear your voice last night on the phone.
   I know you're worried that I'm in danger. Lizzie, I promise to do everything I can to stay safe. We're both wearing our helmets, right? Pinky swear? When I get home, I'll only have to wear a helmet to ride bikes with you and Thomas!

   Can't wait to talk to you again soon!

Mommy

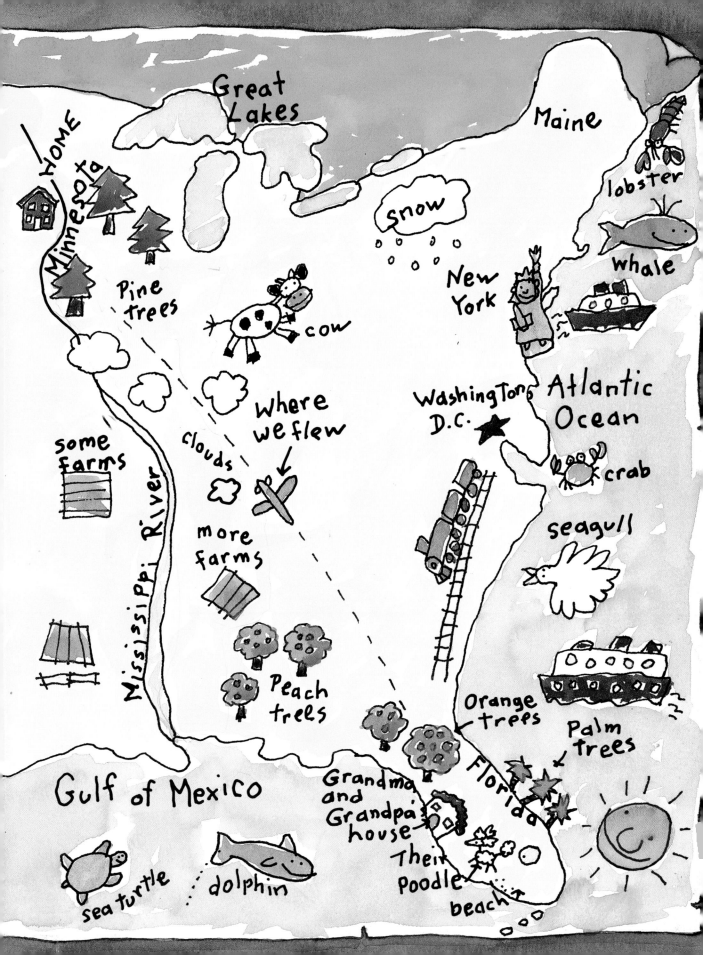

January 2

Dear Mommy,
   I got your letter today. Mrs. Collins showed the class on the map where the troops are fighting.   She said the troops move around a lot, so we can't know exactly where you are.   Mommy, when we looked on the globe, you were almost all the way on the other side! It doesn't look as far on the flat map I made, so I like that one better.
   My class made cards for the soldiers serving with you and with Katie's dad (he's overseas, too), so you'll all have something for the new year. My card has the map of the world with an X on our house.
   Mommy, I know you can't tell me exactly where you are, but I can show you exactly where I am!

   Happy New Year from our cold and snowy state,

   Lizzie

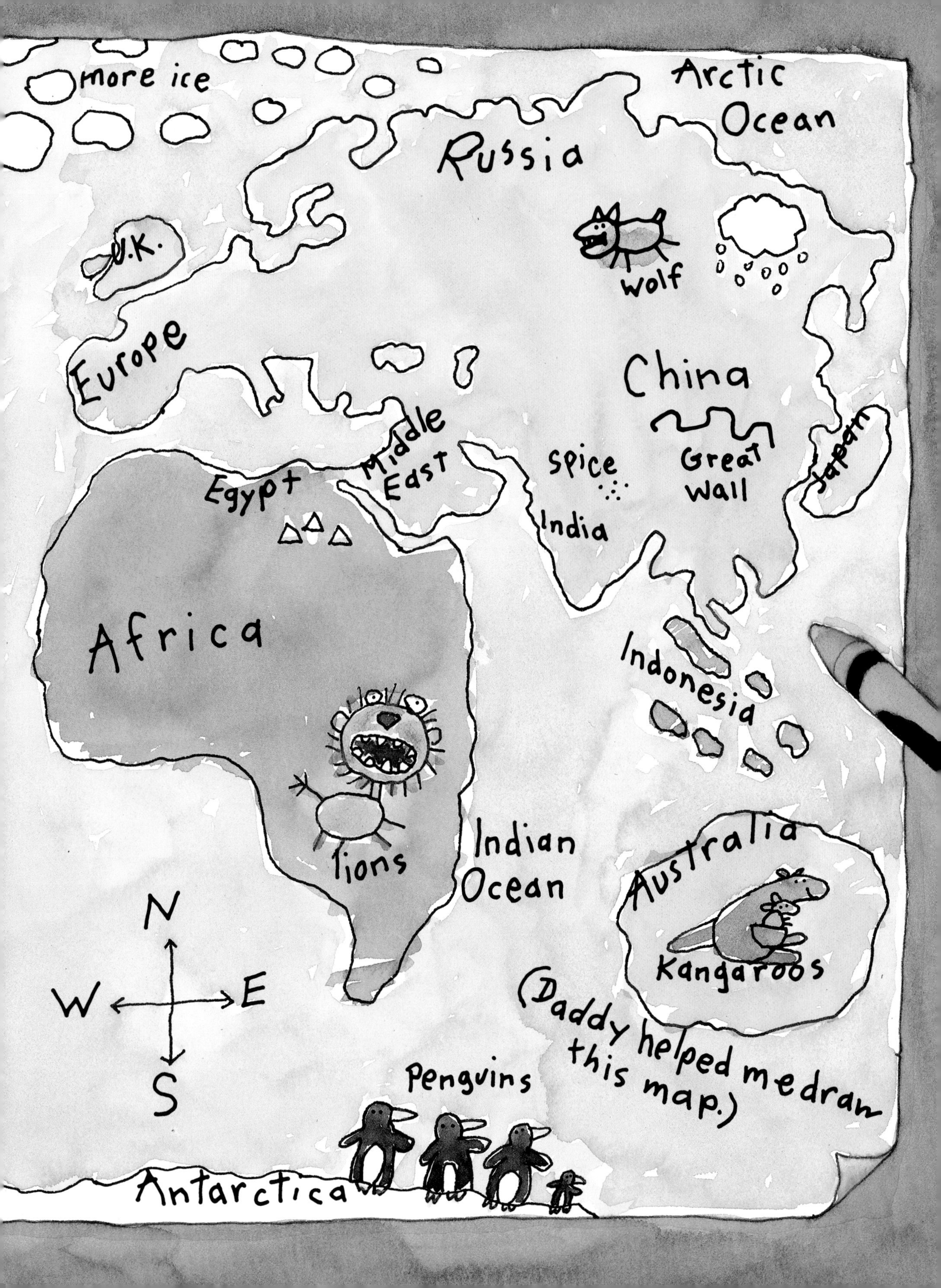
more ice
Arctic Ocean
Russia
U.K.
wolf
Europe
China
Middle East
Egypt
Spice
Great Wall
Japan
India
Africa
Indonesia
lions
Indian Ocean
Australia
Kangaroos
N
W
E
S
(Daddy helped me draw this map.)
Penguins
Antarctica

March 9

Dear Mommy,

I really missed you on my birthday today. Sarah came over for a sleepover and Daddy made a cake and Thomas sang that I looked like a monkey and I smelled like one, too. I put the card you sent where I can see it when I wake up.

Daddy gave me the telescope you asked him to get me — thanks! You said you and I see the same stars, even though when it's lunchtime here, it's nighttime where you are. Daddy said to send you a star map and tell you which star to look at so that we can both make a wish on it!

So, Mommy, make a wish on the bright North Star. Use the Big Dipper to help you find it, like you showed me, and look for the Little Dipper, too. Hey! They're sort of like you and me!

Your big birthday girl (that's what you called me in the card),

Lizzie

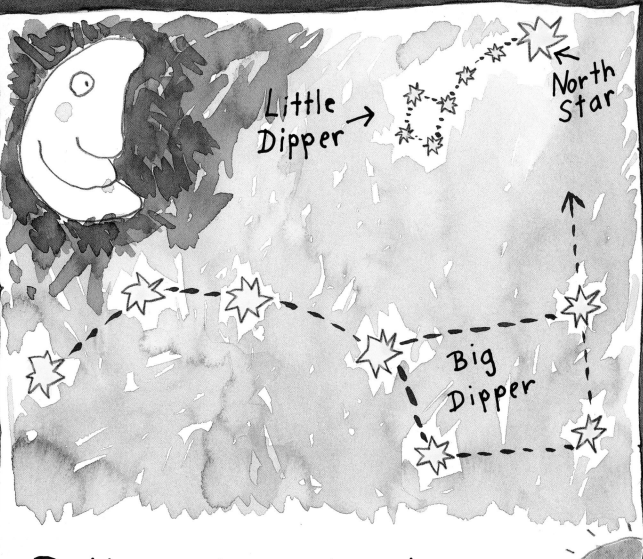

Little Dipper →

North Star ←

Big Dipper

Daddy said the sun is a star, too. If the sun were the size of my head, Earth would be the size of the pupil in my eye.

If Earth is so tiny, then you're not far away at all!

Me

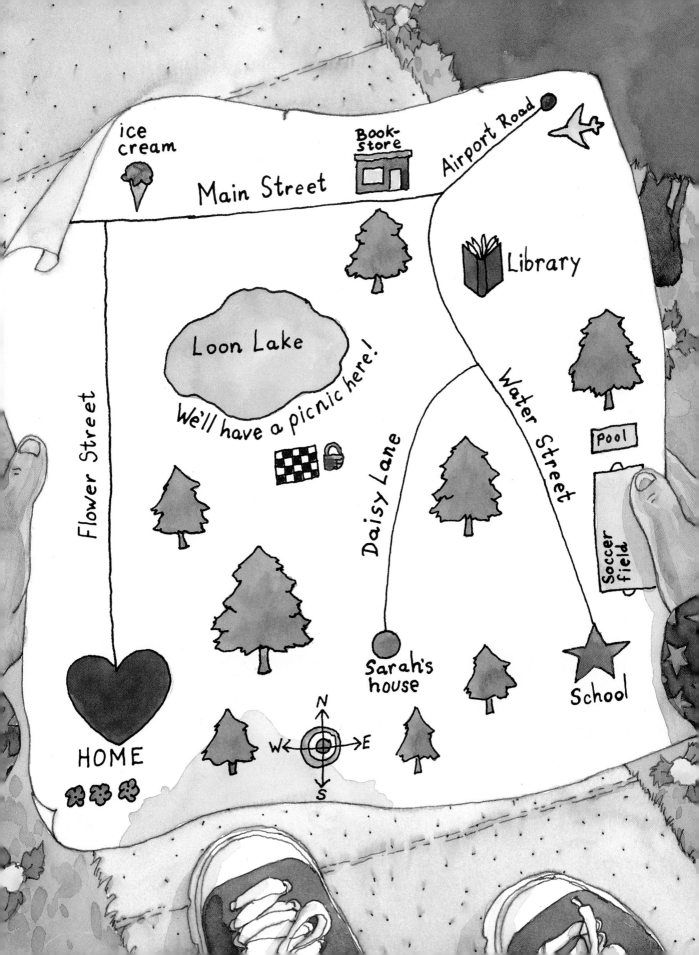

When a Parent Is Deployed: Tips from Lizzie and Her Mom on Handling the Separation

Although it was hard, Lizzie and her mom stayed close while Mommy was overseas. Lizzie's dad did a great job of helping Lizzie keep in touch. If your family has a parent overseas, here are some tips to help kids through what can be a difficult time.

★ **Plan ahead.** If you know that you're likely to be deployed, be sure to talk about it as a family ahead of time. Children need a lot of time to process separation, so the more they know in advance, the better.

★ **Make sure that your child has lots of physical reminders of you.** Children of deployed parents love to look at photos and memory books, just as Lizzie benefited from seeing the photo of Mommy in her helmet and boots. Many kids like to listen to tapes of mom or dad reading a bedtime story. A calendar marked with important dates ("Mom's birthday," "Dad's deployment date," "Thanksgiving") can help kids keep track of the days until you return.

★ **Keep your routine as regular as possible.** Although the "Mommy's away" routine might be different from the one your family follows when Mom's around, kids thrive on predictability and schedules. The more they know about what to expect each day, the better they'll adjust. Lizzie knew that Daddy and Mrs. Cooperman would take good care of her and that she'd go to school, play in soccer games, and otherwise have a normal daily life.

★ **Be straightforward when talking about safety.** Even very young children can understand that a deployed parent may be in danger. While parents will want to reassure their children that they are doing everything possible to stay safe, just as Lizzie's mom did, they will also want to allow children to express anxiety, especially those who are old enough to be aware of the nature of military conflict. A good approach is to tell children that you plan to come home and to describe the measures your unit takes to stay safe.

★ **Connect with other military families.** Lizzie was helped by knowing that Katie's dad was overseas, too. If your child has the opportunity to socialize with the children of other deployed parents, he or she will feel more normal and connected. What's more, the parent at home can really benefit from meeting other spouses as well!

★ **Take advantage of the programs the military offers.** The Armed Forces offer Family Readiness programs to help military families. Services include arrangements for phone calls, email, video conferencing, free babysitting, car maintenance, and pillowcases for kids with photos of their deployed parents. Lizzie and her mom stayed closer when they were able to email and phone each other and exchange photos and gifts.